Produced by The Creative Spark
San Clemente, California

Illustrated by Yakovetic Productions

Written by M.C. Varley

Printed in the United States of America.

ISBN 1-56326-150-2

A Charmed Life

Somewhere under the sea, in a place far, far away, the Little
Mermaid had a secret grotto filled with treasures from the human world.
There were dinglehoppers, and snarfblatts, and even a whatsit
or two. Ariel loved to go there every day, just to admire
her beautiful things.

Sometimes her friend Scuttle the seagull would bring her new things, and today was no exception.

"Ahoy, Scuttle!" Ariel called out excitedly as she reached the surface.

"Ahoy, Ariel! You'll never believe what I found!" cried the bird as he came in for a landing. "It's the most unusual leaf I've ever seen! And I want you to have it."

"Scuttle, you've found a four-leaf clover!" Ariel gasped.
"A four-leaf clover? Wow, how about that?" said Scuttle. "What's a four-leaf clover?"

"It's a good luck charm, you silly gull," laughed Ariel. "I read about it in a book. Humans say it brings good luck to anyone who has one, as long as that person takes good care of it."

"You have to show that to Sebastian and Flounder right away!" said Scuttle.

And so the Little Mermaid quickly swam away to find her friends.

"Wait until you see the wonderful present Scuttle gave me!" Ariel said when she found Sebastian and Flounder.

"And wait until you see what I found buried in the sand!" Sebastian the crab replied, holding out a crystal goblet. "You must have lost this during our picnic."

"It really works!" Ariel cried, taking the goblet from Sebastian.

"What really works?" asked the little fish, Flounder.

"My new lucky charm! See? It's a four-leaf clover. Humans say that it brings good luck."

Sebastian scowled. "Good luck, indeed. Don't tell me you believe all that nonsense?"

"Don't you?" asked Ariel.

"No, I don't. It's just a silly superstition," said Sebastian. "Humans may believe that four-leaf clovers bring good luck, but I don't."

"Then how do you explain finding my missing goblet?" Ariel asked.

"Coincidence," the little crab said with authority. "I just happened to find it at the same time, that's all."

But Ariel liked the idea of having a lucky charm, and so she tucked the little clover safely away inside the pages of her book.

Over the next few days, Ariel's luck did change. She found her lost necklace, and discovered a sunken ship to explore filled with all sorts of treasures. Sebastian continued to say it was all just coincidence.

"Wow," Flounder said, "she sure is lucky to have all these coincidences!"

But what Ariel didn't know was that Ursula the Sea Witch had heard about her good fortune, and had discovered where she kept the lucky charm.

"A book's not a very safe place to keep such a valuable charm," Ursula sneered. "You never know when a strong current might come up and wash that little clover out of the pages."

One day Ursula waited until the
Little Mermaid and her friends were
nowhere in sight, then entered the grotto.
She swirled her tentacles around faster and
faster until the pages of the book began to turn.
The little clover rose with the current and landed
between Flotsam and Jetsam, Ursula's evil pet eels.

Ursula quickly scooped up the charm. "Finders keepers," she said with an evil laugh. "Right, boys?"

Ariel didn't notice the clover was missing until the next morning. "Oh, no!" she cried, "What am I going to do?"

"Maybe it just fell on the floor or something," Flounder said. As they started to look, Ariel knocked over her crystal goblet, breaking it into little pieces.

"Now look what happened! Without my lucky charm, I'll have nothing but bad luck forever!"

Sure enough, Ariel's luck seemed to change overnight. By the next day she had broken three more glasses and lost her bag of gold doubloons. "This is terrible!" she cried.

"Poor Ariel," Flounder said. "If only I could find her another four-leaf clover, it would make her lucky again." Then he had an idea. He decided to make a four-leaf clover out of seaweed and pretend to Ariel that it was her lost lucky charm.

Meanwhile Ursula, who had the real four-leaf clover, found Ariel's bag of lost doubloons, which had fallen behind some rocks outside the grotto.

"This is my lucky day!" the sea witch exclaimed.

Flotsam and Jetsam tried to reach the gold, but the opening was too small. "Fools!" Ursula screamed, pushing them aside. "Out of my way!"

She stuck a slippery tentacle into the tiny opening, but as she did the rocks came crashing down on her head. "Lucky charm, indeed!" she growled.

After Flounder gave Ariel the seaweed clover, her good luck soon returned. She found three pearls and two shiny buttons and she even found the bag of lost gold doubloons Ursula had tried to take. She was sure she owed it all to her lucky four-leaf clover.

"Something about this doesn't look quite right," Sebastian said, examining the clover closely. "Have a look for yourself."

Ariel twirled the clover in her hand, looking at it from all sides. "Why, you're right! This isn't my clover! It's just a piece of seaweed! Flounder! Do you know anything about this?"

The little fish turned red as an anemone. "I was only trying to help," he said in a small voice.

"I don't understand," Ariel said. "When I thought this was the real clover, everything was so perfect."

"Now you've got it," replied Sebastian. "It's what you think in your mind that counts. When you believe in yourself, good things can happen. There's nothing magical about it."

"Does that mean you're going to throw that fake clover away now?" Flounder asked.

"Of course not!" said Ariel. "I'm going to keep it forever, to remind me that I shouldn't rely on a clover for good luck. I can rely on myself to make good things happen."